The Eleventh Hour

A Curious Mystery

Graeme Base

A book is read, a story ends, a telling tale is told.
But who can say what mysteries a single page may hold?
A maze of hidden codes and clues, a clock at every turn,
And only time will tell what other secrets you may learn . . .

For Robyn
And for my parents

Puffin Books

When Horace turned Eleven he decided there should be
Some kind of celebration. 'For my friends', he said, 'and me.
For though I've been the age of eight and nine and six and seven,
This is the very first time that I've ever been Eleven!'

With that he set to work and wrote the name of every Guest,
And then eleven sorts of food that Elephants like best.
He wrote the Invitations next (and sent them off that day),
And finally eleven Games for everyone to play.

Now Horace was a clever lad; he planned the day with care,
Ensuring that his party would be quite a Grand Affair.
But only in the Kitchen was his genius unfurled,
For Elephants are verily the best cooks in the world.

He started off with cheesecake full of strawberries and cream,
Then moved on through the pastries to a Chocolate Supreme.
And though it may be said, perhaps, that Horace made a mess,
The Feast that he created was Fantastic, nothing less.

'Twas early in the morning when the Party Guests arrived
And each was wearing Fancy Dress most artfully contrived.
The Pig came as an Admiral, the Zebra as a Punk.
The Rhino was an Astronaut, his spacesuit made of junk.

The Swan arrived as Princess Pure, a most enchanting sight,
Bejewelled with rows of precious stones and dressed in purest white.
And with her came an Indian, with arrows, spear and bow –
A handsome Bengal Tiger, whom no one seemed to know.

The Mouse came as a Musketeer, his head and hat held high,
A swagger in his footsteps and a twinkle in his eye.
The Cat was Cleopatra, Queen of Egypt and the Nile,
And, masquerading as a Judge, was Sam the Crocodile.

And then there was a pair of twins – two sisters, both Giraffes,
Who turned up dressed as Angels and received a round of laughs.
Their haloes shone upon their heads, two shiny golden rings,
And from their nylon tutus sprouted painted cardboard wings.

The Guests were met by Horace as they stepped into the Hall
(He'd dressed as a Centurion of Rome Before the Fall);
And once inside they looked around and noticed with a smile
The way the Hall had been designed in High Renaissance style.

No sooner had they entered than a rumour filled the air,
And stopped the conversation as the news spread everywhere.
Their Host had made a Banquet! It was huge! Immense in size!
And one by one the Guests were drawn within to feast their eyes . . .

For there upon the table was The Feast That Horace Made,
A wondrous spread of cakes and buns and jugs of lemonade.
And in its midst a Centrepiece of Grand Design was placed,
That left no doubt young Horace had superb artistic taste.

But if the Guests had hoped to eat the Banquet there and then,
They soon found out their Host had plans for what they'd eat and when,
For Horace told them firmly not a crumb would they devour,
Until the time that he had set – THE ELEVENTH HOUR.

The Games began at 8.05 – a sack-race marked the start,
With sacks of every size and shape, so everyone took part.
They set off at a cracking pace, with Eric to the fore,
But close behind the others hopped, on trotter, hoof and paw.

They raced across the Croquet Lawn, then up towards the house,
But as they reached the half-way point the Pig tripped on the Mouse.
He landed with a heavy thud, and several others fell,
But Kilroy kept his balance, and went on to win, as well!

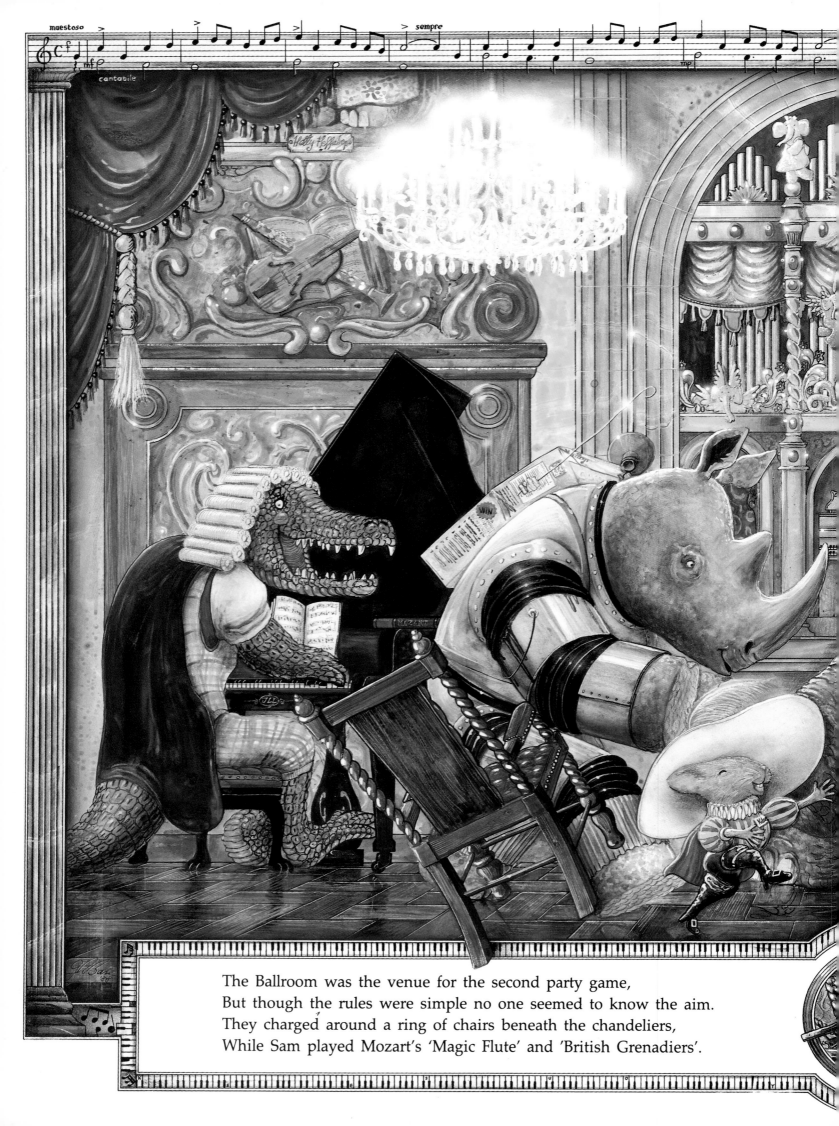

The Ballroom was the venue for the second party game,
But though the rules were simple no one seemed to know the aim.
They charged around a ring of chairs beneath the chandeliers,
While Sam played Mozart's 'Magic Flute' and 'British Grenadiers'.

And one by one the chairs became just piles of splintered wood,
(The Guests were all agreed that this new game was jolly good!)
Then as the final chair collapsed they stopped and checked the score;
And since no one had won at all, they settled on a draw.

The Pig procured a pack of cards and soon a game began.
But unbeknown to all the rest the Admiral had a plan,
For Oliver won every trick; his conquest was complete.
A string of luck? Or could it be the porker was a cheat?

A little later in the day some Guests played Snakes and Ladders,
Upon a board that squirmed and turned with Pythons, Asps and Adders.
The board was set, the race was on, the game had just begun,
Then Thomas went and ate the dice, so no one ever won.

A Cricket Match was organised for those who knew the game –
The twin Giraffes had no idea, but fielded just the same.
But Oliver, a Boastful Pig, had made it understood
That when it came to batting he was really rather good.

The Tiger donned the keeper's gloves and crouched behind the stumps,
And waited for a chance to show his skill at leaps and jumps.
The Pig went for a mighty swing, but only clipped the ball,
And Maxwell leapt, and caught him out. Pride comes before a fall.

The Cricket Match had finished when the Zebra took his cue
And challenged tiny Kilroy to a game of Pool or two.
But Kilroy's skill was quite immense for somebody so small –
Though Eric thought he'd win hoofs down, he didn't pot a ball.

The other Guests enjoyed a lively game of Blind Man's Buff,
With Piggy in the Middle (you would think he'd had enough!).
He blundered blindfold round the room and groped and grabbed and gripped,
While all the others squealed with joy, and dodged and ducked and dipped.

A Tennis Match was under way a little later on,
With Crocodile and Tiger versus Elephant and Swan.
The Elephant was shaky: it appeared he'd lost his nerve.
The score was 40/30 with Crocodile to serve.

Sam tossed the ball into the air then struck it with such force
That Horace didn't see it start upon its fateful course,
And sure enough it hit poor Horace square upon the head.
'Game, Set and Match', the Tiger cried. 'That's life', poor Horace said.

And meanwhile, midst Egyptian columns, row on silent row,
A Seeker searched while others Hid – a game that all will know.
But though her eyes were large and bright, the Cat's success was small,
For while she searched with utmost care, she found no one at all.

And far above, upon a hill beyond the Tennis Court,
The Rhino and the Zebra sat in silence, deep in thought.
They studied every Rook and Pawn, each King and Queen and Knight,
Then both agreed it looked too hard, and quit without a fight.

The final game was Tug o' War – two teams of equal weight –
But every mind was on the feast, the time was getting late!
The Rhino slipped, the game was lost, they cared not in the least!
For finally the Hour had come – 'twas time to eat the Feast!

'My friends', said Horace to his Guests, 'my friends, lend me your ears!
For now it is that I, your Host, have reached Eleven years!'
But if he planned to make a speech, his virtues to espouse,
He missed his chance, 'coz everyone took off towards the house!

They raced each other up the stairs (Eleven steps in all),
Then past the marble statues leading to the Banquet Hall.
And there they stopped. No body spoke. They stood in disbelief.
For all the food had disappeared. Aghast, they cried: 'A Thief!'

The cakes had turned to scattered crumbs, no cream was to be seen,
And nothing now remained where once the Chocolate Mousse had been.
The Centrepiece had toppled, not a strawberry was left.
'But who', they cried, 'could possibly have managed such a theft?'

The Zebra said, 'It wasn't I!
By All my Stripes, I'd rather die!'
The Tiger said, 'It wasn't me!
I've far too much integrity.'
Then Cora cried, 'It wasn't us!
We wouldn't dare cause such a fuss.'
And Kilroy squeaked, 'I'm far too small;
One mouse could never eat it all!'

The Swan looked darkly at the Pig,
'The Thief must be someone who's big!'
But Oliver denied all guilt,
And said, 'Now Thomas, he's well built.'
The Rhino sobbed, through sniffs and tears,
'I've known our Host for years and years,
And though my appetite is large,
I must deny this dreadful charge.'

With manners fine or poise uncouth, Yea, all who seek take heed forsooth, For everyone has told the truth!

The Cat had yet to say a word,
Which Eric thought could be inferred
As Prima Facie evidence
Of Feline Guilt *re* this Offence.
But Alexandra lashed her tail,
'Your theories are to no avail!
We Cats do *not* steal others' food.
It's wicked, bad and *very* rude!'

The Judge was next: 'I too deny,
Although I have no alibi,
All blame for this horrendous crime . . .'
(He waffled on for quite some time.)
'I'm not the kind of Crocodile
To fake a tear or force a smile.
My countenance is plain to read;
My friends, I did not do this deed!'

The Mystery was Curious! The Guests were at a loss,
But Horace had initiative; he showed them who was Boss.
'The Feast is gone, we can't change that, but now it's clear to see
That what we need is cheering up – just leave it all to me.'

He rushed into the Kitchen and was gone for quite a while,
Then re-emerged with sandwiches, a flourish and a smile.
'This lot is not as fancy as the Birthday Feast', he said,
'But eleven times as healthy, 'coz it's made with wholemeal bread!'

Then, as they sat and ate their lunch, there came one last surprise,
When Horace asked for everyone to kindly close their eyes.
And there it was – the Birthday Cake! The Guests all clapped and cheered.
He'd kept it in the Kitchen, and it hadn't disappeared!

And so they picnicked on the lawn until the evening fell,
And everyone left satisfied – the day had finished well.
But in the end, although the thief was someone they all knew,
They never found out who it was that stole the feast – can you?

THE THIEF WAS SOMEONE THEY ALL KNEW

Notes for Detectives

With a little close observation and some simple deduction it is quite easy to discover which of the eleven animals stole the feast. Look carefully at the pictures, and when you think you know who it was, use the first letter of that animal's name to decode the panel below.

Here's what to do. If you think the thief was, say, Maxwell, then call 'M' the letter A, and go on through the alphabet so 'N' equals B, 'O' equals C and so on. In this way you can decode the hidden message below, which will tell you who stole the feast and, more importantly, how it was done.

MYXQBKDEVKDSYXC ! SD GKC SXNOON USVBYI
DRO WYECO GRY CDYVO DRO POKCD. LED RO
RKN ROVZ : YXO REXNBON KXN OVOFOX YP
USVBYI'C PEBBI BOVKDSFOC RSN DROWCOVFOC
SX DRO RYECO KXN KBYEXN DRO QKBNOX KXN,
KD OVOFOX WSXEDOC DY OVOFOX DROI KVV
CMKWZOBON SXDY DRO LKXAEOD RKVV GSDR USVBYI
KXN KDO EZ KVV YP RYBKMO'C LOKEDSPEV PYYN.
KXN XYG, TECD DY CRYG RYG MVOFOB IYE KBO,
MKX IYE PSXN YXO REXNBON KXN OVOFOX WSMO
RSNNOX SX DRO ZSMDEBOC ? RKZZI REXDSXQ !

THE INSIDE STORY

Within lies the solution to the Curious
Mystery of The Eleventh Hour, as well as detailed
explanations of all the clues and puzzles in the
illustrations. Do not turn this page until you
have tried your hardest to unravel the Mystery – *for the
getting of wisdom is no match for the thrill of the chase, and
those who choose the longer road shall reap their reward!*

Graeme Base

The Inside Story

In writing *The Eleventh Hour: The Inside Story* I wanted to do a number of things. Firstly, I felt obliged, having set so many puzzles, to provide a list of answers to them in the interests of fair play. Secondly, I suspected that a few of the clues might remain hidden to many readers and I wanted to give a complete explanation of every message and its meaning. Thirdly, I have in several instances borrowed architectural designs and decorative devices from various places in Europe, Asia and Africa, which I thought should be pointed out and acknowledged.

By the time you read this booklet you will probably have discovered, by one means or another, which of the eleven animals at Horace's birthday party stole the Feast. You will also have located and, I hope, deciphered most of the clues hidden within the book and decoded the final page with its revelation of how the Feast vanished. If you have not done these things, *do not read any further!*

There are several ways of finding out who stole the Feast. The easiest is, of course, to concentrate on the final page, breaking the code either by obscure cryptographical means or by the simple expedient of trying the first letter of each animal's name in turn. (It is clearly stated in the 'Notes for Detectives' on the final page of the book that the thief is one of the eleven animals and not some other unknown or obscure character.)

The second method is that of observation and deduction. A careful examination of the pages reveals that the time of the theft can be pinpointed to within a minute or so. With this information in hand, it is a simple matter for those with good eyesight and powers of recognition to deduce which of the eleven is the thief.

Method three involves the numerous messages hidden throughout the book. To arrive at the correct answer by means of these often misleading and frustrating snippets of advice and information, it is necessary to differentiate between statements that are true and those that are half-truths, sort out which messages offer clues and which merely confuse the issue, and ignore the apparent in favour of the obscure. A little knowledge of ancient Egypt could also prove useful.

And last, but not least, there is the leap of intuition (or patently obvious conclusion) that in a book that revolves around the number eleven you need only look as far as the eleventh letter of the alphabet.

What follows is a page-by-page guide to every clue, reference, allusion and red herring that I intentionally incorporated in the pictures of the book.

The Illustrations

Horace's Study

The main message in this first picture starts in the left-hand bottom corner and runs clockwise around the pencils in the grey border. It reads DRAWING CONCLUSIONS FROM SKETCHY CLUES MAY LEAD YOU ASTRAY, SO SHARPEN YOUR EYES AND YOUR WITS – GET THE POINT? Despite the painful puns, the message does offer some good advice: don't trust the clues – just use your eyes and head.

But the border holds a more direct clue: in the decorative white rectangle on each pencil there is a letter and, reading clockwise once more, you will find another message – IT WAS NOT MAX. You can thus eliminate the Tiger from your list of suspects.

The notice-board in the top left corner holds an important clue as well: a rough sketch for the illustration of the Hide and Seek game, a picture which later turns out to be crucial for budding detectives.

The copy of *Animalia* is there purely for the purpose of self-advertisement!

The Kitchen

Only one clue is to be found in this page, and that is in the letters scattered about on the door of the refrigerator. When they are grouped according to colour and unjumbled, the message reads IT [green] WAS [yellow] NOT [blue] HORACE [red].

The initials FK on the blue book on the shelf are those of a friend of mine who is a great cook!

The Arrival

The guests arrived at Horace's house at 22 minutes to 8, as the digital clock on Eric's motor scooter shows. The number plate E.11 is not significant, unlike the letters in the wrought-iron gates, which read WATCH THE CLOCKS, suggesting that time may play an important part in the forthcoming mystery. (It is no coincidence that the final line of the verse on the title page stresses the importance of time.)

The strange logo on Oliver's skateboard, which also appears on a badge on the notice-board in Horace's study, is just a device I sometimes use as a secret signature on pictures. The giant Panda symbol on the motor scooter is the World Wildlife Fund's logo.

The Entrance Hall

The sumptuous Entrance Hall is based on the interior of St Peter's, Rome, although I've added a few elephanty bits here and there.

The message of the illustration stands out clearly on the golden panels above the archways, and if it is not immediately obvious that each group of letters is an anagram, this can be established by carefully following the titles around the border in a clockwise direction, starting at the bottom left-hand corner. I may have confused the issue somewhat by writing TICK and TOCK at either end of the message. Sorry! These are just there to make you think about the clocks in the illustrations. The black message reads ONE MOUSE COULD NEVER EAT IT ALL. The red message in the middle reads KILROY SPEAKS THE TRUTH, but woe betide those who take the message at face value. Kilroy does not lie, but neither does he tell the whole truth.

The words 'Maintain Your Rage' in the grey cameo between the verses will be recognised as a reference to another curious mystery, which took place on 11 November 1975 – the dismissal of the Australian Government.

The Feast

Looking decidedly mediaeval, Horace's Banquet Hall is loosely based on the interior of several castles in England and Scotland. The picture contains a number of messages. The main one starts in the bottom right-hand corner and runs anticlockwise around the border; it reads CAN YOU FIND A HIDDEN MESSAGE IN EVERY ILLUSTRATION? Other messages can be found in two of the banners that flank the archway. In the banner on the left the blue letters read, from left to right, OBSERVATION, and the red letters say DEDUCTION. The white message reads DO NOT GUESS, while in black there is the word TICK. In the right-hand banner blue reads NOW YOU SEE IT (turn to my discussion of 'The Feast Vanishes' for the rest of the saying). Red says LOOK CAREFULLY, and white reads WATCH THE CLOCKS. Black says TOCK, thereby completing another timely reminder.

The Sack-race

There is only one message here and it is fairly obvious. Across the sacks the top lettering says OBSERVATION and the bottom lettering follows with & DEDUCTION, because in the book I wanted you to try to deduce the identity of the thief by looking carefully at the pictures rather than by taking short cuts or just guessing.

Musical Chairs

In Salzburg there is a palace called Schloss Mirabell, and in this palace is a room where the young Wolfgang Amadeus Mozart often played the piano for the aristocracy. The lavish golden decorations of the room were the inspiration for my Ballroom (although the pipe organ, minus elephants, comes from a church many kilometres away in Copenhagen). Having borrowed from this room for the picture, it seemed only proper to have Sam playing music from Mozart's *The Magic Flute* on the grand piano. Sam's other party piece, 'The British Grenadiers', appears in musical notation along the top of the border, but it is the lower notes, which form a slightly cacophanous counterpoint, that prove the more interesting. The tune? Why, it's 'Three Blind Mice'! (And Kilroy does seem quite in keeping with the melody as he rushes gleefully forward, with eyes closed and no sign of a tail!)

This clue is a real give-away for the musically minded, but if reading music is not your forte, look to the very bottom of the picture and read, from right to left, the tiny letters along the keyboard decoration, which say SAM IS NOT THE ONE YOU SEEK. The initials JLL on the piano are those of my sister-in-law, Jenny, who helped by expertly scoring the musical clue for me. Incidentally, the design of the chairs comes from some I saw at Chatsworth House in England.

The Card Game

Glasgow, on the west coast of Scotland, was the home of an architect and designer called Charles Rennie Mackintosh. Among his many inventive designs were some extraordinary, high-backed chairs upon which our four card players now perch. The setting is a mixture of art nouveau and art deco, with some glassware pieces reminiscent of Lalique and pottery like that of Clarice Cliff, but all this means little to Eric the Zebra who can't understand why he is losing every hand. The reason, I'm afraid, is that Oliver the Pig is indeed cheating. Follow his eyes and you can see how. The Zebra's cards are being reflected in the mirror on top of the cupboard!

This discovery is actually the key to solving the difficult code of cards that runs along the top of the page. The backs of Eric's four cards read C, O, D, E. By looking in the mirror we can see that the faces of those cards are $3\heartsuit$, $2\clubsuit$, $4\heartsuit$ and $5\heartsuit$, so c=$3\heartsuit$, D=$4\heartsuit$ and E=$5\heartsuit$, giving us the clue that the first half of the alphabet is found in the thirteen cards of the suit of hearts and ends with M=K$\heartsuit$. Since O=$2\clubsuit$ we can expect the second half of the alphabet to follow the suit of clubs, starting with N=A$\clubsuit$.

The card code is probably the hardest puzzle in the book. The decoded message reads THE PIG IS A CHEAT, BUT NOT A THIEF. Oliver is in the clear.

The cards to the sides of the verse can now easily be decoded as TICK TOCK once again. The letters on the vase covered in pink fish read, appropriately enough, RED HERRING, but if you tilt the book away from you and squint along the page, with your nose right down on the paper, you will find a very strong clue in the curtains. The left-hand curtain can be made to read ALL FOR ONE, and the right-hand curtain AND ONE FOR ALL, echoing the famous creed of the Three Musketeers. The meaning will become clear when you study the costumes of all the guests.

The Snakes and Ladders Game

The rug comes from Turkey; I have the original hanging on my living room wall! The Snakes and Ladders board was copied from a very old one belonging to my wife Robyn's grandmother.

The clue lies, as you might expect, in the board game, and can be found by examining the yellow squares. The numbers on these squares don't follow the sequence of numbers running from zero to 100 up the board, but appear to be quite random. If you work out the code from the hint given in the middle of the border above the verse (A=1), then read the yellow squares from top to bottom, you will find the message THOMAS IS INNOCENT.

If you wish to know the time, refer to the area near Thomas's left leg.

The Cricket Match

A typical English village green comes to mind in this scene, especially as cricket is such an eminently English sport. The lovestruck carving in the boughs of the old tree provides the key to decoding the message on the cricket balls spaced around the border. It reads A=Z and Z=A, so B=Y, C=X, and so on. This reversed alphabet code reveals the information GIRAFFES DO NOT STEAL.

The Pool Game

My English background is again evident in the decor of the Pool Room, as is my tendency to awful puns in the solution to the code on this page. The simple number code is the same as the one in the Snakes and Ladders page, but this time it runs anticlockwise around the border, starting in the bottom right-hand corner. It reads TAKE MY CUE, POOL YOUR RESOURCES, AND DON'T BE SNOOKERED BY BASELESS SUSPICIONS. This means very little, I admit, but as compensation try playing join-the-dots with the pool balls. Join the numbers from one to eleven, and see what letter you come up with. (May I suggest you use tracing paper rather than ruin the book?)

The tail of the Tiger and the shadow of Thomas passing by the open door may well have aroused your suspicions, but the two guests are just heading to the Nursery for a game of Blind Man's Buff.

Blind Man's Buff

To unravel the lines of dots and dashes in the larger border of the illustration you will need to find a copy of the Morse code. The solution is actually a riddle:

THE TWO GIRAFFES ARE INNOCENT,
ENTIRELY FREE OF BLAME,
WHICH LEAVES US WITH THE MYSTERY
OF CORA'S SISTER'S NAME.

In the border surrounding the verse you will find this hint:

THE ANSWER TO THIS EXTRA RIDDLE
LIES NEAR PIGGY IN THE MIDDLE.

(And there is also the familiar TICK TOCK to the left and right of the verse.)

Now, if you turn your attention to the bingo board you will find yet another number code, which in fact will provide you with several useful pieces of information. Call A one, B two, C three, and so on, and the message reads KARNAK HOLDS IN SHADOWY SILENCE THE SECRET YOU ARE LOOKING FOR [space] GO YE AND SEEK IT.

If you knew that Karnak was a huge and ancient temple complex in Egypt, you would immediately turn to the Hide and Seek page and examine it closely. If, however, you didn't know anything about ancient Egypt, you could still further your investigations by noticing that when the left-hand column of decoded letters on the bingo board is read from top to bottom a significant clue is revealed.

And finally, the riddle in Morse code can be resolved, if you isolate the decoded letters in the pink squares of the bingo board and arrange them according to the small numbers to the right of each row. You will find that the other Giraffe's name is CLARICE. (I took the names Cora and Clarice from identical twins created by Mervin Peake in the *Gormenghast* trilogy.)

Other obscure clues are scattered near the bingo board: the name on the side of the tip truck, the stripes on the beach ball, and yet another TICK TOCK on the building blocks.

The Tennis Match

It takes very little time to realise when studying this picture that each of the tennis balls has a different letter on it. It also takes relatively little time to discover that, by taking each ball in turn from left to right, you can read RED HERRING.

To find a more useful clue may take a little longer and will require turning the book upside down. Then you will find, spelt out in the trunks of the bushes in the shrubbery just behind the tennis players' feet, the words WATCH THE WINDOWS.

If you then turn the book right way up again and follow the advice of the shrubbery, you will notice a most important fact. The Feast is visible through the windows and is clearly still all in one piece. The Cat can be seen peeping over the bushes, the twin Giraffes are visible and the Pig can also be seen some way off.

Make a note of the time on Sam's pocket watch, then turn to the next page . . .

Hide and Seek

In the days when Egypt was ruled by the pharaohs, the capital city was Luxor. Just a few kilometres from this city stood the incredible temple complex of Karnak. Although now in ruins, it still remains a most awe-inspiring sight – much more mysterious and impressive than my little row of columns! Nevertheless, this Karnak-inspired picture does hold some mysteries. Indeed, it is the central illustration of the book. It has been alluded to twice already, once on Horace's notice-board and again in the message of the bingo board.

The ancient Egyptians used a form of communication called hieroglyphics, which I have utilised to create the code in the picture. The column of hieroglyphs running down the left-hand border relates directly to the stylised alphabet running down the right-hand border. I must admit that in some instances where there was no hieroglyphic equivalent to a letter, I made one up: an apple to represent A, an egg-cup for E, three figures in a row for Q, a teacup for T, and a few others as well.

Using this key you can decode the various messages in the Hide and Seek picture. Each word in the border at the top and on the columns is enclosed in a rounded shape called a cartouche. The four cartouches across the top of the page read ALEXANDRA IS NOT GUILTY. The border above the verse says PUT NO TRUST IN HIDDEN CODES AND MESSAGES, the words to either side read TICK TOCK, and the strip below translates as WRITING IN HIEROGLYPHICS IS DRIVING ME NUTS. The three cartouches at the top of the nearest columns on both sides together read SEEK AND YE SHALL NOT FIND (the meaning of which will become clear shortly). All the other cartouches on the columns say HIDE and SEEK.

But look at the picture itself more closely. Alexandra is the central character as she searches for the other animals. We can see the Pig peeping out from behind the columns, and the Giraffes also. In the background the four tennis players are visible, and way up on the hill are the silhouettes of Eric the Zebra and Thomas the Rhinoceros. There is only one character you will not find in this scene, hence the cryptic clue 'Seek and ye shall not find'.

The Cat's golden collar and the head-dresses of the statues are based on jewellery worn by King Tutankhamun over 3000 years ago. I called the Cat Alexandra after the Egyptian city of Alexandria.

The time is 11 minutes to eleven.

The Chess Game

The setting for the Chess Game, reminiscent of the intricate red stone carvings that adorn many buildings in Rajasthan in northern India, contains a good clue for anyone who has studied Latin or knows a lot about small mammals. Around the central arch of the summerhouse are the words MUS MUSCULUS DOMESTICUS. On the left and right arches appear the words TICK and TOCK.

A clue that relies somewhat less on specific knowledge can be found along the edge of the chess table in the form of various boxes and angled lines. By relating these shapes to the arrangements of the alphabet given on either side of the verse, it is possible to decode the message. For instance, the first shape, a square on a light background, represents the letter E, the next shape is R, and the third is I. The complete message reads ERIC IS NOT THE THIEF.

But all this is unimportant compared with the discovery that is to be made by looking closely at the house in the distance. The Feast that was clearly visible just moments ago in the Tennis Match picture has vanished, and the Centrepiece of Grand Design is lying on its side in the window. Look carefully for all the animals. You will find all but one.

So there you have it. At 10.48 in the Tennis Match picture the Feast is still there. At 10.49 in the Hide and Seek illustration one character is missing and at 10.50 in the Chess Game picture the Feast has vanished. Every character is accounted for during the crucial minute or so except for one and we can therefore deduce that he or she must be the thief.

The Tug o' War

This is the eleventh and final game played at Horace's birthday party. The letters carved in the wall around the door should be read backwards, as the writing on the ceiling of the porch indicates, but they only say ANOTHER RED HERRING. The real message can be seen in the window when you hold the page up to a mirror. It reads TIME WILL TELL.

The cameo between the verses also holds a little clue. Considering who came first in the Sack-race, it is surprising to see who is coming last up the stairs at 11 o'clock!

The Feast Vanishes

In the Banquet Hall the crime has been discovered. Around the border the message has changed to:

GOODNESS GRACIOUS, HOW AUDACIOUS
SOMEBODY WAS MOST VORACIOUS.

The two banners also have new messages. In black (this time reading down the rows of both banners) are the words THERE IS ALWAYS A SHORT CUT, in red THOSE WHO CHOOSE THE LONGER ROAD SHALL REAP THEIR REWARD!! and in white the ubiquitous TICK TOCK. Reading across the right-hand banner, you will find in blue the second half of the old saying 'Now you see it': NOW YOU DON'T.

Excuses and Accusations

Hold the book up to a mirror and you will find this six-line poem:

NOW HEARKEN EVERY WOULD-BE SLEUTH

OF TENDER YEARS OR LONG IN TOOTH
THE ANCIENT SAGE, THE KEENEST YOUTH
WITH MANNERS FINE OR POISE UNCOUTH
YEA, ALL WHO SEEK TAKE HEED FORSOOTH
FOR EVERYONE HAS TOLD THE TRUTH!!

And so it is, for no one has lied but, to be sure, not everyone has told the whole truth.

The Sandwiches

Horace bursts out of the Kitchen with a huge plateful of sandwiches to replace the lost Feast. The profound words written across the doorway are there merely to assist in unjumbling the simple message in the border around the verse. By putting the first letter of each word last and the last letter first, the message reads:

DON'T BE MISTAKEN, DON'T BE MISLED,
TRUST NOT IN MESSAGES, JUST USE YOUR HEAD.

It's what I've said all along.

The Picnic

With this final page the story ends happily, though not entirely satisfactorily. It is significant that the animals' faces are all visible except one.

The final message is taken from the last verse and is written across the bottom of the border. The letters of the words are the right way round and in the right order but disconcertingly spaced. When the words are properly spaced they read THE THIEF WAS SOMEONE THEY ALL KNEW.

The Last Page

The solution given in the panel, when decoded, reads:

CONGRATULATIONS! IT WAS INDEED KILROY THE MOUSE WHO STOLE THE FEAST. BUT HE HAD HELP: ONE HUNDRED AND ELEVEN OF KILROY'S FURRY RELATIVES HID THEMSELVES IN THE HOUSE AND AROUND THE GARDENS AND, AT ELEVEN MINUTES TO ELEVEN, THEY ALL SCAMPERED INTO THE BANQUET HALL WITH KILROY AND ATE UP ALL OF HORACE'S BEAUTIFUL FOOD.

AND NOW, JUST TO SHOW HOW CLEVER YOU ARE, CAN YOU FIND ONE HUNDRED AND ELEVEN MICE HIDDEN IN THE PICTURES? HAPPY HUNTING!

In case you were wondering, the tiny R that appears somewhere in every illustration is not a clue; it stands for Robyn, to whom the book is dedicated.

I hope you found *The Eleventh Hour* entertaining and intriguing. If you also found it annoying and frustrating, this booklet was written especially for you! And now, for your further annoyance, just one final question: did you ever find out the name of the Swan?

Locations of the Mice

Almost every picture in *The Eleventh Hour* contains at least one hidden mouse. The actual number of mice concealed in an illustration is given by a number in a circle somewhere on the page. Here is a list of where the mice are on every page of the book.

Horace's Study (number ⑱ is inside the cupboard): all eighteen are grouped together in the stained-glass window fanning out from the centre in pink and green.

Kitchen (number ③ is on the refrigerator door): one is in the border, near the bottom right corner; one is in the green mixing bowl; and one is on Horace's ear.

The Arrival (number ⑦ is on the motor scooter's handlebars): one is in the border, four bricks down from the top right corner; in the gates, two are above WATCH, one is near Pig's foot, two are above THE and one is below Crocodile's mouth.

The Entrance Hall (number ⑦ is on the loose tile, lower left): one is in the border, under the ninth tile, top right; two are on Tiger's jacket; one is in the foliage seen through the window; one is above Swan's head; one is below Zebra's hoof; and one is under the sign 'To the Banquet Hall'.

The Feast (number ⑥ is in the left-hand suit of armour's shoulder): one is in the border, above the fourth plate from the bottom left corner; one is under the pink dessert with wafers; one is against the giant spoon's handle; two are on the right-hand suit of armour's breastplate; and one is in the centre cameo.

The Sack-race (number ⑥ is in the centre cameo): one is in the border, bottom left; one is in Horace's armour; one is under Crocodile's chin; one is on Kilroy's sack; one is on Cat's sack; and one is on Pig's red sash.

Musical Chairs (number ⑧ is in the border, lower right): one is under Hetty Heffalump's portrait; one is in Horace H. Heffalump's portrait; one is in the back of the central blue chair; one is under Horace's feet; one is on the far right blue chair; one is below Rhino's ear; and two are in the central cameo.

The Card Game (number ③ is in the lower left corner): one is on the blue vase; one is on the cupboard above Zebra; and one is on the wallpaper under the far right lamp.

The Snakes and Ladders Game (number ③ is in the border, lower right): one is in the left border; one is in the top border; and one is on Zebra's right leg.

The Cricket Match (number ⑥ is in the centre cameo): one is in the branches above Horace; one is in the tree above the heart-shaped carving; one is below Zebra's right hoof; one is on Tiger's jacket; one is in the border near Tiger's tail; and one is in the border, top left.

The Pool Game (number ⑤ is in the border, around the verse): one is on Zebra's singlet; one is in the carving beneath Kilroy; and three are on the grandfather clock.

Blind Man's Buff (number ③ is on the elephant soldier's hat): one is on Tiger's jacket; one is on Horace's helmet; and one is on the leg of the easel, lower left.

The Tennis Match (number ⑦ is in the bottom left corner): one is in the net; one is on Tiger's leg; one is on Crocodile's left hand; one is in the branches above Crocodile's hand; one is in the branches, far left; one is on Horace's right leg; and one is in the border, top left.

Hide and Seek (number ④ is on the leaf above the signature): one is below the right-hand statue's head-dress; one is in the lower left corner; and two are in the Cat's head-dress.

The Chess Game (number ③ is in the border, below Rhino's foot): one is in the chair near Zebra's leg; one is in the carving, behind Rhino; and one is in the carving, top right.

The Tug o' War (number ⑦ is on Crocodile's face): one is on Crocodile's left foot; one is in Horace's breastplate; one is on Horace's leg; one is on Tiger's leg; one is on the roof tiles, top left; one is on the elephant statue, fourth from right; and one is in the tree trunk, far right.

The Feast Vanishes (number ⑥ is in the right-hand suit of armour's ear): one is in the top border, near the centre; one is on the right-hand suit of armour's right arm; and four are in the green banner, top left.

Excuses and Accusations: there are *no* mice hidden in this page!

The Sandwiches (number ① is in Horace's breastplate): in the grain of the door, lower right.

The Picnic (number ⑧ is in the border, left of the verses): three are in the trunk and branches of the gum tree; three are in the bushes near the ladybird, lower right; and two are in the bushes, lower left.

And one for luck.